BLACKWATER

Blackwater is a cold, dark thriller with a twist.

Davey has always lived in the shadow of his older brother, who will stop at nothing to protect himself and his family. But when Denis Tanter comes into Davey's life, how far will they go to get him out of it? Can you really count on your brother to watch your back?

Conn Iggulden is the number one bestselling author of the Emperor series.

BLACKWATER

Conn Iggulden

BBC
LARGE
PRINT

First published in 2006 by
HarperCollins Publishers
This Large Print edition published
2006 by BBC Audiobooks by
arrangement with
HarperCollins Publishers

ISBN 1 4056 2185 0
ISBN 13: 978 1 405 62185 4

British Library Cataloguing in Publication Data available

Printed and bound by CPI Antony Rowe, Eastbourne

BLACKWATER

To Matthew Arpino,
who swam the Welsh lake

CHAPTER ONE

I stood in the water and thought about drowning. It's strange how the sea is always calmer at night. I've walked along Brighton beach a hundred times on cold days and the waves are always there, sliding over and over each other. In the dark the water is smooth and black, with just a hiss of noise as it vanishes into the pebbles. You can't hear it in the day, over gulls and cars and screaming children, but at night the sea whispers, calling you in.

The swell pulled at the cloth of my best black suit, reaching upwards in the gentle rise and fall of unseen currents. It felt intimate somehow, as if I was being tugged down and made heavier. Even the icy Brighton wind had grown easy on my skin, or perhaps I'd just gone numb. If I had, it was a welcome numbness. I'd spent too much time thinking and now there was just the final choice of walking into a deeper dark.

I heard the crunch of footsteps on the shingle, but I didn't turn my head. In dark clothes, I knew I would be almost invisible to the dog walkers or late night revellers, or whoever else had braved the cold. I'd seen a few pale figures in the distance by the pier and heard high voices calling to each other. They didn't touch me. There was something wonderful about standing in the sea, fully clothed. I'd left the land behind me, with all its noise and light and discarded chips in lumps of wet paper. I tasted bitterness in my mouth, but I was free of fear and guilt, free of all of it. When I heard his voice, I thought it was a memory.

'Now how bad can it be, to have you standing out there on a night like this?' he said. My older brother's voice. I could not help the spasm of nervousness that broke through my numb thoughts. I had been there for hours. I was ready to walk into the deep water until my clothes grew heavy and I could empty my lungs in a sudden rush of bright bubbles. I was ready, and his voice pulled me back, just as securely as if he had cast a line that snagged on my jacket.

'If you go in now, you'll drown us both,' he said. 'I'll have to follow you, you know that.'

'And maybe just one will come out,' I replied, my voice rough. I heard him laugh and I couldn't turn to face him. I'd feared him all my life, and if I turned I knew I'd have to look him in the eyes. I heard him chuckle softly.

'Maybe, Davey boy. Maybe it would be you.'

I thought of a boy we'd both known, a lad with a cruel streak a mile wide. His name had been Robert Penrith, though even his mother called him Bobby. I can see her face at his funeral, so white she looked as if she was made of paste. I'd stood at the side of a damp hole in the ground watching the box being lowered in and I remember wondering if she'd ever known how her son had terrorized us.

He liked humiliation more than pain, did Bobby. His favourite was the simple thing of forcing you down to the ground with your legs right over your head, so pressed that you could barely take a breath. When he did it to me, I remember his face reddening with mine, until I could feel my pulse thumping in my ears. Even as young as I was, I knew there was something wrong with the way he grew so hot and excited. As a man, the thought of being so helpless makes me want to scratch myself.

I think my brother killed him. I'd never had the nerve to ask outright, but our eyes had met as the coffin dropped down into the hole between us. I hadn't known how to look away, but before I could he'd winked

4

at me and I'd remembered all the secret cruelties of his life.

Bobby Penrith had drowned in a lake so far north of Brighton it was like another world. My brother had dared him across on a day when the water was so cold it turned the skin blue. My brother had made it to the other side, to where we waited in a shivering group. He climbed out as if he was made of rubber, flopping and staggering before leaning on a rock and vomiting steaming yellow liquid onto his bare feet.

I think I knew before anyone else, though I stared past him with the others, waiting for a glimpse of Bobby's red scalp coming doggedly in. It took divers to bring him back in the end, beaching his body three hours later, with the lake busier than the tourist season. The police had interviewed us all, and my brother had been in tears. The divers had cursed with all the anger of men who fished for dead children on bitter days. We felt their scorn like blows as we shivered in rough red blankets.

I'd listened while my brother told them nothing worth hearing. He hadn't seen it happen, he said. The first he knew of the tragedy was when he reached the far bank alone. I might have believed him if he hadn't seen Bobby hurting me only the day before.

You never really know when a story starts, do you? Bobby had decided I deserved a special punishment, for breaking some rule of his. I'd been crying when my brother came by and Bobby let go. Neither of us was sure what he might do, but there was a hard tightness to my brother that even lads like Bobby found frightening. Just a glance at his dark eyes and a face that looked a little white over the bones and Bobby had dropped me straight away.

The two of them had looked at each other and my brother had smiled. A day later and Bobby

Penrith was cold and blue on the side of Derwentwater. I didn't dare ask the question and it had settled inside me like a cold lump. I felt guilty even for the freedom it brought me. I could walk past Bobby's house without the usual terror that he would see me and fall into step at my side. The boy had an evil streak in him, but he was not a match for my brother and only a fool would have tried to swim on a November day. Only a boy who had been frightened by an even bigger fish than he was.

In the utter darkness of the Brighton shingle, I began to shiver with the cold. Of course he noticed, and I heard a note of amusement in his voice as he went on.

'They say suicides don't feel pain. Did you ever hear that, Davey? They cut and cut away at themselves, but they're so wrapped up in their own heads that the cowardly little shits barely feel a sting. Can you believe that? It is a strange world.'

I hadn't felt the cold before. I thought it was numbness, but now it seemed to hit me all at once, as if the wind was tearing right through the skin. My hidden feet were aching with a cold that gnawed up the bones of my legs. I crossed my arms over my chest and I felt it all coming back to me. I would have given anything for numbness then. The alternative was terror and shame.

'Are you going to tell me why my brave little brother would be out standing in the sea on a cold night?' he went on. 'The wind is freezing the arse off me, I can only imagine what it must be like for you, Davey? I'd have brought a coat if I'd known.'

I felt tears on my cheeks and I wondered why they weren't turning to ice with the cold that pierced me.

'There are things I can't bear any more,' I said, after a time. I didn't want to talk about it. I wanted that fine and simple mood I'd been in when he arrived, when I was calm.

8

My bladder had filled without me noticing, and now it made itself felt. Every part of me that had been ruled by my misery now seemed to have woken and be screaming for attention, for warmth. How long had I been standing there?

'I have an enemy,' I said softly. There was silence behind me and I didn't know if he had heard me or not.

'How deep are you in?' he said, and for an insane moment I thought he meant the water.

'I can't handle it,' I said, shaking my head. 'I can't . . . I can't stop it.' More tears came and at last I turned to face the man my brother had become. His face was still stretched over his bones and his hair was a dark bristle over pale skin. There were women who thought him handsome to the point of compulsion, though he never stayed long with one. It seemed to me that his cruelty was there for the world to see in that hard face and watchful eyes. I was the only one who thought this. The rest of the world saw what he wanted them to see. He had brought a coat, I noticed, despite his words. His hands were dug into the pockets.

'Let me help,' he said. The moon gave enough light to see the rising shingle behind him. A million tons of loose stone at his back should have made him insignificant, should have reduced him. Yet he was solidly there, as if he'd been planted. No doubts for the man my brother had become. No conscience, no guilt. I'd always known he was lacking that extra little voice that torments the rest of us. I'd always been afraid of it, but when he offered, I felt nothing but relief.

'What can you do?' I said.

'I can kill him, Davey. Like I did before.'

I could not speak for a long, slow breath. I hadn't wanted to know. My mind filled with images of Bobby Penrith flagging as he swam in freezing water. My brother was a fine swimmer and it would not have taken much to hold him under, to exhaust him. Just a flurry of splashing and then the smooth strokes towards the shore, arriving as if exhausted. Perhaps he had been. Perhaps Bobby had struggled and fought back with all the strength of desperation.

I looked into my brother's eyes and saw all of the years between us.

'Tell me,' he said.

CHAPTER TWO

Denis Tanter was not the sort of man to frighten you on first meeting. In fact, when I was placed at his table during a New Year's Eve party I hardly noticed him at first. He was short and compact, like a featherweight boxer. He'd been one in his twenties, I discovered later, and he still had the posture and freckled skin that flushed easily. He had a good grip, and red hair, which was just about all I took in before I was pulling crackers and trying to remember how I'd ended up sitting with strangers on a night meant for family. I didn't see him as a threat and he really wasn't at that point, not to me. I've met a lot of men like him over the years and they usually dismiss me after the first brief clasp of hands. I'm not one of the breed, or something. They rank me as harmless and move on. I could leave more of an impression if I tried, but I just can't make myself care about the little rituals of life, especially between men. Maybe that has hurt me.

My wife Carol was doing her usual social duty with the other wives, sounding each other out on income, children and education. I've seen attractive women who can raise female hackles up to fifty yards, but Carol slips under the radar, somehow. She always dresses with a bit of class and she's one of those who seem to be able to match earrings with a bracelet so there's always a polished feel to her. God save us from beautiful women. They have too many advantages.

Once or twice I've caught the end of one of her private smiles, a glance or wink, or some more subtle signal that says 'at least we understand' to a complete stranger. It works to disarm women, but it also works on men. I usually see it coming, from the casual touching and standing a little too close to seeing them drive past me as I walk home. There's nothing quite so depressing as peering into a car as it goes by in the rain. There used to be arguments. Once, when I still cared enough, I struggled with a man on wet grass until he scrambled away, leaving me with a broken nose. It's amazing how sticky blood is when it's on your hands.

I wouldn't have chosen the marriage for myself, not like that. We used to scream at each other, and twice she locked me out of the house. Maybe I should have left, but I didn't. Some people just don't, and I can't give you a better reason than that. I loved her then. I love her now. I know she's scared of a thousand things—of growing old, of having children. I tell myself she takes these men into our bed when she can't bear herself any longer and that sort of lie helps more than you might think. These days I just don't ask her about the nights she spends away. I don't let her come to bed until she's washed the scent off her, and somehow we get by, year after year. I love her and I hate her, and if you don't know how that works I really envy you.

When I was twenty-two I went with Carol to a club in Camden. I've known her forever, you know. My brother was with us and he had a pretty thing named Rachel on his arm, a girl who danced every Saturday at the club. She wasn't paid for it, but they had a raised stage there and no one objected to the sight of her moving as well as she did.

That club was almost completely dark and heavy with heat and music. Whenever you thought you could catch a breath, a dry ice machine would kick in and the dance floor would fill with choking whiteness.

We got ourselves drunk on large bottles of Newcastle brown ale, and when the right tune came on we climbed onto that raised section to join her. It was larger than I realized and there were people against the wall behind us as we stamped and cheered. It was hotter than you'd believe and I had my shirt off, but I was slim enough and young enough not to give a damn what anybody thought.

Some of that evening goes and comes in flashes, but I do remember my brother's girlfriend whipping her hair round and round next to me, so that it struck my chest and shoulders hard enough to sting. I loved it.

A man came out of the shadows by the back wall and asked Carol to dance. He was short and slim and swayed slightly as he stood there. I could see he was drunk and I didn't think he was a threat, just as I missed Denis Tanter on that first night. Maybe that's my problem. I just don't see these people coming.

Carol shook her head in that sweetly apologetic way she has and pointed to her loving husband, spoken for, sorry, you know how it is. He stared where she pointed before shrugging and turning away. That should have been it.

I didn't realize anything was happening until I was struck on the back of the head. Have you ever been knocked with very little force and had it hurt like you were on fire? There are pressure points all over your body, like little traitors to your self-esteem. The way that drunk hit me was the exact opposite. I felt it had been really hard, but somehow it didn't hurt at all. I looked around in confusion, thinking I had been bumped by someone passing by. The little bastard was standing directly behind me, his eyes shining in the strobe lights. It was Carol who shouted over the noise of the music that he'd tried to butt his head into mine.

He was completely blank with drink, and as he grinned at me I suddenly couldn't bear it. I shoved him in the chest with both hands and he fell flat at the feet of a dozen strangers. I remember thinking that if he got up I'd have to jump down from the stage and lose myself in the crowd. I don't fight people in clubs. I refuse to be ashamed of the fact that I don't enjoy the rush of panic adrenalin the way others seem to.

My heart was beating so fast that I felt light-headed and ill. Acid came into my mouth and I swallowed hard, wincing. Carol came to stand at my shoulder and the pair of us looked down at him. He still looked harmless as he lay sprawled and his grin never faltered. Even then, even though he'd gone for me already, I didn't think he was dangerous.

My brother had managed to miss all the excitement with a trip to the bar. By the time he returned, Carol and I had moved quietly to one side of the little stage, with a solid wall to our backs. I've said I didn't think he was a threat, that little man, but I didn't want to dance with my back to him, either. My brother didn't know anything about it, of course. He passed out the drinks and carried on dancing and whooping with the crowd. God, we were young then. He'd taken off his shirt as well, even prouder of his wiry frame than I was of mine.

I saw my attacker coming out of the darkness. My brother was dancing where I had been dancing and he was dressed almost exactly the same. The man smashed a bottle over the base of his skull and the two of them hurtled off the stage to the dance floor, parting the crowd as they fell.

I froze for a moment, and I'm not proud of that. It felt like the music had stopped, but of course it hadn't. Carol screamed and then I moved, jumping down and grabbing hold of two slippery bodies, locked together. My brother had been taken completely by surprise, but as I heaved at them he was grunting and fighting like a madman. I could see the whites of their eyes and bared teeth. The pair of them were straining at each other's flesh with desperate strength. I couldn't break my brother's grip. My hands slipped on the skin, and to my horror I realized there was a *hell* of a lot of blood coming from somewhere. There was broken glass everywhere and beer and blood on my hands. I reached down again, and at that moment the dry ice machine kicked in. Thick fog filled the dance floor and we all went blind.

I strained to take a breath, terrified that I was going to be punched or cut while I couldn't see. I still had a hold of slippery skin, and somewhere below me they continued to gouge at each other in a frenzy, causing as much pain and damage as possible.

I heard the bouncers coming at last and there were pointing hands and shouting people everywhere. I felt strong arms pull me away. God knows where Carol had gone to at that point. I didn't blame her for getting clear of it. I blamed the evil little drunk that the bouncers threw out of a back entrance.

My brother was lifted to his feet looking like a wild man. He was dazed and covered in trails of blood right down his bare chest. The bouncers took him to their own bathroom somewhere in the back of the club, and I went with him to wash the muck off my hands. It really is amazing how blood can gum up your fingers. Even a small amount can go further than you think.

We were alone in that echoing bathroom and I felt like an actor behind the stage. The music had continued right through what happened and we could still hear the thumping rhythms, though they were far away. All right, I hadn't been involved, but I'd been afraid and I was bloody. I felt like I'd survived a battle. Away from the crowds and the danger my spirits rose quickly enough, even when I saw the gash in his neck from the bottle. It seeped sluggishly, producing a dark, heavy trail that would not be staunched.

He looked at it in the mirror and I saw how pale he'd gone.

'We should get you to hospital, for stitches,' I told him. He was still stunned and I didn't want him to ask why he'd been attacked by a maniac for no reason. I knew it should have been me and I felt enough relief and guilt to be light-headed.

When he turned to me, I could see he was raging. I handed him a wad of toilet paper for his neck.

'He could have killed me,' he said, dabbing at the wound while he stared back at himself in the mirror. 'Where did he go?'

'He'll be long gone by now,' I replied. 'The bouncers threw him out.' He shrugged, pulling on his shirt over the pad of tissues. He swore as he saw his trousers had been gashed and that there was more blood staining the cloth.

'He owes me,' he said.

I followed him out.

*   *   *

He should have gone home, that man, whatever his name was. He shouldn't have been standing at a bus stop only fifty yards from the club. That was his second mistake of the evening, and sometimes just one can get you killed. When he saw my brother stalking towards him, he should have run, he really should. Instead, he just grinned the same soft grin, like he didn't have a care in the world.

My brother hit him hard enough to

put him down, cutting his knuckles on the man's teeth. Then he kicked him as he lay there, twice before he even curled up. I should have stopped it then. Hell, I should have stopped him leaving the club and just insisted on taking him to hospital. I didn't, though. I wanted a little revenge as well. I could have been killed that evening. I'm not proud of it, but there was a debt to be paid.

Another kick to the head and it should have been over, but two more muted thumps kept him down. I couldn't see the man's face, and I didn't want to. I was slow holding my brother back, but in the end, when it was late, I did. I take comfort from that. I am not him, even when I'm full of anger and spite. I am not. He would have kicked that man to death. Maybe he did.

We left him there on the pavement and I did take my brother to hospital to be stitched and flirted with by a nurse. I read the next day's papers looking for news of a killing in Camden, near the Underworld club. There was nothing.

*   *   *

When we met Denis, Carol still drew men in when she was hungry, though she'd learned a few things about keeping them at arm's length as well. For years I hadn't had to deal with one of her hangers-on, those peculiar males who would pretend to be a caring colleague or a friend while they waited for her to fall into bed with them. It was usually enough to have a quiet word, just to let them know I knew. I didn't need help until we met Denis Tanter. Even then it might have been enough to turn a blind eye to a few afternoons in hotels until she had scratched her itch.

You think the first time is going to kill you, but it just doesn't. The night is the worst one of your life, but when sleep does come it turns off your imagination. You wake up the next day and she's there making breakfast and everything is all right again. I could have lived with that, I *knew* I could. The problem with Denis Tanter was that he wanted Carol all to himself.

CHAPTER THREE

Do you know what gives one man power over other men? You'd think it would be money, or some high position, being a judge perhaps, or a politician. In all honesty, when are you ever troubled by that kind of level? I've never had the Foreign Minister turn up at my door and insist I move my car. I think if he did I would probably call the police. I'm not saying they don't have power, of a kind. Of course they do—too much of it, maybe. It just isn't the sort of thing that presses you down on a daily basis. You don't have them come into your house and take your wallet, if you see what I mean.

There is a lesser place, though, underneath the courts and security guards, right down where it can really tear the spleen right out of you. It doesn't take an army and it certainly doesn't take enormous amounts of money. For just a few hundred pounds a week, one man can hire another one to punch and kick and break, maybe even to rape or rob, if that was needed. Just *one* man to do whatever he's asked. That's all it takes. I can only imagine what it must be like to have one.

Men like Denis Tanter spend a pleasant evening in a restaurant, and by the time they get home, someone they want to frighten has had his door kicked in and his fingers broken by a complete stranger. You can't go to the police because you know they'll make it worse the second time. You know that fear is usually enough. Most men aren't able to stop one violent criminal holding them down and battering their head so hard on the kitchen tiles that they break. Most men care about a woman, or a child, something that grabs them and squeezes their chest in terror if they're even mentioned.

You don't get fear like that from politicians or judges. You know they have limits, no matter what happens. If you walk free out of court, you don't expect the police to send men round to your house that night to give you a bit of justice.

I'd actually met Denis's man, Michael, at the New Year's Eve party. He wasn't enormous, like those bouncers you see on club doorways. Denis had found himself a solid, six-foot boxer without a single moral to trouble his conscience. I even chatted to Michael that first evening, and I think I should have had some sort of warning, some instinct. Life would be a lot easier if we felt a shiver down the spine when we met a man who will be punching us unconscious a month later.

I realize now that he stopped me at the bar because Denis was talking to Carol. Just one man on the payroll makes that sort of thing easy. Just a quick word and the husband loses almost an hour in strained small talk with a complete stranger. I even had a tray full of drinks, but every time I started to go back Michael dropped one of his hands onto my arm and made some comment, or joke, or asked me some inane question. I remember he said he had put on a bit of weight over the winter, but come spring, when he was 'in season', he would turn it back into muscle. I'd never heard anyone describe themselves that way before. It wasn't exactly politeness that kept me there, it was a prickling fear that he was drunk and he was violent and I didn't want to offend him. I stood it as long as I could, and when he turned away at last to pick up his change from the barman, I walked back to the table.

Carol wasn't there and neither was Denis. It's so easy now to understand what had happened, but at the time I just didn't. Midnight was coming and I had the drinks in. I sipped one pint to the dregs and then started on another when she was suddenly back at the table and Denis was there too, kissing his wife just as the countdown started. You wouldn't think I could miss something like that, knowing what I did, but I've stopped that sort of paranoia. It eats you alive, especially if you're right every now and then. You really can't watch them all the time. It destroys your nerves, your stomach and maybe your sanity.

Carol did look a little flushed, I remember. I put it down to alcohol and excitement. Balloons came down from the ceiling and everybody joined hands with strangers and sang that Scottish song where you only know one line and everyone repeats it over and over. There was a man in a kilt there and I remember smiling when I saw him and turning to Carol to see if she'd noticed. She smiled back at me and everything was all right.

31

*　　　*　　　*

The thing that really makes me bitter is that poor old Denis didn't know the woman he was dealing with. If he'd gone hard at her like he did at his business acquaintances, he'd have had her skirt up after a meal or two. The trouble with Carol is that she looks the complete opposite. If you can imagine a Grace Kelly with dark hair, it isn't her at all, but the *attitude*, the long neck and pale skin, that's the same. She's the sort of woman you want to muss a little, to see a tendril of hair come loose and a wicked gleam come into her eyes. You know the type? She's the sort of woman you want to gasp when you kiss her. I worked hard at it when we were young together. She was a little drunk that first time with me. It wasn't the way I'd pictured it. I could hardly see her in the dark room back at the student halls. Her thighs were long and white and they made a whispering sound as I ran my hand down them. I remember that she cradled my head against her, almost like holding a child. I think one of us cried, but we were drunk and young and it was a long time ago and two different people.

Denis thought he had found the great love of his life, of course.

*   *   *

Carol sells houses to people with too much money, the sort of people who surround themselves with gold-framed pictures and match the colour to their bath taps. Denis wouldn't have looked out of place on her client list, even if he'd brought Michael as a driver. I heard his name when a girl from Carol's office left a message about taking 'Mr Tanter' to another viewing. I didn't recognize it at first, but there was another one the following day. I pressed the buttons on the phone and I heard the girl's voice—with him in the background, making a wisecrack. I think I probably knew then, as I wiped the message. Carol hadn't heard it yet, but I just wanted it off the phone memory, as if I could wipe away my suspicions with a couple of quick clicks.

She hates me when I think something is going on. She says I pretend to be normal and friendly, but all the time there is a spite in my eyes that she can't bear. She says it makes her want to get out of the house. Sometimes she does and comes back smelling of drink and too much perfume at two or three in the morning. When she's drunk, I pretend to be asleep. If she sees I'm awake, she talks like a gutter whore and it's all I can do to lie there and pretend I can't hear every last word of it. It's just another one of the little games we play with each other.

I think it took Denis about a week

to ask her to come to a hotel with him. It might have been sooner if he'd known her, of course, but I think he probably felt like the luckiest man in the world as she dropped her skirt to her ankles and stepped out of it. I've been on the receiving end of the best she has to offer, and it caught me. I mean, I'm still here after some pretty vicious years, so I can sort of appreciate what Denis went through, you know? I'm not saying I understand the man. He was a taker and I knew it from the first time I met him. Like my brother, he was one of those people who use those around them, for fun, for sex, for friendship.

Sometimes they make a mistake and think they've found something more important than it really is. Denis did that with Carol, the moment he woke up in the hotel and found out she'd gone. She'd come home to me in the small hours and Denis was not the sort to understand that kind of relationship. Hell, *I* don't understand it and I'm in it.

She came home to me because she always comes home to me. She doesn't stay till the morning, not after they've gone to sleep. After all, a hotel morning is just bad breath, crumpled clothes and a full English breakfast with too much salt and burned coffee. To be honest, I don't really care why she trusts me enough to keep coming back. Maybe she even loves me as much as I love her.

That great love of hers didn't stop it happening again, of course. I don't know whether it was another hotel, or maybe even his own house. The difference from my point of view was that the second time she spent an evening away that week, Denis arranged for me to have a friendly visitor. While he was bending Carol over a bed somewhere plush, I actually opened the door with a piece of buttered toast in my hand. Can you imagine anything more middle class and harmless? I had a mouthful of bread and Marmite as I recognized Michael and I was in the middle of trying to say something when he took a step forward and shoved me onto my back. I think he trod on one of my feet first, but I didn't take much in as I smacked my head on the hall floor. If it had been carpeted I might have been a little sharper for the next few minutes. Unfortunately it was block wood, and one of the things that sold us the house when we first saw it.

It was the casual nature of it that was so insulting. I think most of us have wondered how we would handle a burglar, say, if we confronted one. I thoroughly enjoy politicians talking about 'reasonable force' for those moments in life. You can take it from me that terror makes a mockery of anything resembling reason. I opened the door with some vague thought about a football match on the television. A moment later I was half-stunned and blinded by the hall light directly above me. I felt a hand grab my shirt collar and I found myself sliding along the wooden floor towards the kitchen. I panicked and tried to get up, but I wasn't wearing shoes and my socks slipped underneath me. I couldn't do more than make kicking motions in a panic.

There's a small table and chair in the kitchen. It's too cramped really, but Carol insisted on being able to use the words 'breakfast room' for when we sell the house on. It is her business, after all. That's the sort of stupid thought that came into my head as Michael dragged me up and dumped me on my own chair. Reasonable force? I'd like to see one of them try it with Michael resting his great fists on my kitchen table.

'What do you want?' I said.

'Have you got whisky?' he said. I nodded, and out of habit I half rose to get it.

He pressed a hand on my shoulder, holding me down with no trouble at all.

'You just tell me where,' he said, looking at the cupboards along the kitchen wall.

'By the door, there,' I told him. He would turn and I would reach for one of the knives by the sink behind me.

Instead of following my plan, he reached out and belted me across the face, giving it everything he had. I think I must have blacked out for a while as I lost track of where he was and had to crane my head round, looking for him. He was pouring a little Laphroaig into a glass and everything in the kitchen seemed brighter than usual, like a film.

'Get out,' I mumbled at him, feeling ill. Even as I spoke, I felt the acid come back into my mouth. It's always been the way with me, after some problem with a deteriorating valve. Stomach acid is powerful stuff. I get a blast of it in the back of the throat when I'm frightened or angry, and it burns and burns. There's a name for the valve problem, but the operation is brutal.

'I'm not getting out, Davey. You know that,' he said. I hated him calling me that. My brother and Carol called me Davey, no one else. No one else in my life had known me young enough.

I saw he was wearing black leather gloves to grip the whisky glass. I shook my head to clear it and touched my lips gingerly, trying to feel if they could honestly have swollen as far as they felt. The whole side of my face belonged to someone else. I could only look out of it at him.

'I don't want to be doing this, Davey, I want you to believe that,' Michael said. There was real regret in his eyes, almost a fellow feeling. I hoped to God he wasn't there to kill me.

'Doing what?' I said, terrified. The

40

acid was pooling in my mouth by then, more bitter than vinegar. I wondered what would happen if I spat it into his eyes. Would it burn him the way it seemed to burn me?

'Giving you a little warning, Davey. And drinking your whisky. Telling you to let her go.' He seemed almost apologetic as he said the last part.

'Let who go? Carol?' I said. I wasn't thinking well, with my own blood on the table in front of me. It wouldn't stop dripping out of my nose and I could almost draw loops with it on the pine surface.

'Someone we both know thinks she may be afraid of leaving you, Davey. I think you and I know that's not true. You're not the type, are you, Davey? You're a sensible sort who won't make me have to do something more permanent, aren't you?'

'She won't leave me,' I said, which may be one of the most idiotic things ever to come from my mouth. I should have offered to drive her over

41

to Denis's house in my own car if Michael would have gone. The thought of his house changed the direction of my spinning thoughts.

'What about his own wife?' I demanded. 'I remember her. What does she have to say about it?'

Michael shook his head, as if saddened by all the world's troubles. 'She's left him, Davey. It hasn't been good for a while, and I think your wife was the last straw. He's a free man, Davey. And that's not good for you, I'm sorry to say.'

'You're insane,' I told him. 'You can't just tell a man to leave his wife.'

'Where do you think she is at the moment, Davey? What do you think she's doing?' Michael demanded. 'This isn't like the local vicar's wife, is it? I wouldn't like to imagine what she's getting up to, would you? If I was you, old son, I would leave the bitch and say good riddance to her. What do you want with a woman who takes off like that? We may be doing you a little favour, if you think about it. In the long run, you know.'

My lack of shock seemed to surprise him, and he frowned at me before refilling the glass and corking the bottle. I saw his hand move, but I had hardly begun to duck when the whisky splashed across my face. It burned worse than the stomach acid inside and I yelped, holding up both hands. My eyes streamed with tears and I don't know if it was the fumes or rage at her for doing this to me, for letting these people into our lives. I couldn't think, and when he hit me again I cried out for him to stop, over and over, sobbing.

'You drank a bit too much, Davey, and you fell down the steps outside, catching your face on the ground, something like that. When she asks, Davey, you know. I wouldn't want you telling lies about strange men in your kitchen, would I? You wouldn't want to try and turn her against her new friend with a few whispers, believe me. If she hears I was here, I will show you what I call a second visit, understand? It'll be a lot worse, Davey.' He shook his head slowly, as if imagining it. 'Don't make me come back.'

I was shaking when he left. I drank a little more of the whisky, and by the time she came home the following morning I was still awake and I was drunk and I was raging. I heard her cry out in shock when she saw the wreck Michael had made of my face. Before I could say a word, she was searching in the medicine cupboard for creams and plasters.

'What happened?' she demanded as she sat down in front of me. 'You've been drinking,' came before I could open my mouth. 'Did you fall?' I wondered if Denis had fed her the line, and I winced as my lips cracked. I hesitated just long enough to wonder what would happen if Michael was sent back to make the lesson stick. I didn't have a plan

44

then, I just hadn't fully understood their world. It was too far away from mine.

'Denis Tanter,' I said softly, watching her reaction. She was in the middle of dabbing dried blood out of one of my nostrils and I watched her whole face tighten. Her eyes lost the warm care and tenderness she had been lavishing. Lost it all.

'What do you mean?' she asked, and suddenly I was afraid that the coldness was for me, that she just didn't care any more.

'He had his man come round while you were out last night. You know, to give the husband a little lesson? While you were whoring with his boss. He was warning me off, Carol, making threats in our own *house*.' I heard a tremble in my voice and shut up before the drink brought me to tears.

She looked down at her hands and I could see they were shaking. I couldn't find any sympathy for her.

'That's what you brought into this house, Carol. That's what you did to me last night.'

She'd gone very pale, I saw, as if I'd slapped her. She still held a damp tissue tinged with red. I saw her hand begin to move back to dab at my face and I did slap it away. I didn't think I could bear it if she just went on like nothing had happened. I wanted it all out.

She stood then and her tongue came out to touch the top of her upper lip. She does that when she's really worked up, and I welcomed it. I stood as well to face her, and suddenly the desire for a fight went out of me. I couldn't bear the argument, couldn't stand the words being said again. It was just too much on top of the night I'd had. I'd said them all a thousand times and won the arguments over and over and over. I really didn't actually need to say them aloud to her face. She knew them all.

'Just fix it, Carol. I don't care what happens any more. Just sort it out.'

She nodded, her lips pressed tightly together so that all the blood and colour had gone out of them. I'd never seen her so shaken and, ridiculously, I found it cheering, so that I almost bounced up those stairs to bed. Before she had the shower running, I was asleep.

CHAPTER FOUR

Of course, seeing me sitting there with a bloody nose put Carol in a difficult position. The truth is a strange thing, in case you've never been forced to contemplate its twists and turns. It doesn't matter how bad something is. If you don't admit what's going on, if you don't *say it aloud*, it can be forgotten. It can be managed. It can be ignored. I remember the first time I heard someone joke about 'the elephant in the room'. They meant something that everyone tried to ignore, but who could ignore an elephant? You can take it from me that after a while you hang your clothes on the trunk like he was part of the furniture. You can get used to anything, and as long as you don't actually die, all pain goes. All pain goes. Think of that the next time you think you can't stand it. Think of me. If you don't ask about Bobby Penrith, it's always an accident. Even if you *know*, you just don't force the words out into the open.

You'll appreciate that Carol could hardly wake me up, throw her arms around me and announce that her affair with Denis Tanter was at an end. It was the thing we never mentioned any more, after all. The fact that she rested her head on my pillow was meant to be something I didn't question.

Perhaps because I could feel a tooth wobble when I woke, I just wasn't in a good mood. It must have been twenty years since I last found myself wiggling a loose tooth with my tongue, and it didn't improve my temper. She'd brought it into our kitchen. The old rules were useless until Denis Tanter was out of our lives.

Like it or not, certain things had to be said, no matter how much I hated to do it. I washed myself carefully, looking at the bruises in the long bathroom mirror. I was not a sight to inspire confidence. Even though I felt angry, I looked afraid. Worst of all was the fact that she didn't come back all through the afternoon.

I started thinking she had confronted Denis and tempers had flared. My imagination went a little peculiar for a while. I rang her work because I had to ring someone and ask where she was, though I hated doing it. Every time, I could see their little sly grin on the other end. I was the husband who couldn't find his wife. Have you ever noticed you can hear someone smile on a phone? If you say the same words twice, but smile the second time, you can hear the difference. When you're asking where your wife is, you don't want to hear that change. It starts the brain working fast enough to hurt.

Carol had taken the afternoon off, and there was something in the girl's tone that enjoyed the fact that I didn't know. I had to work to keep my voice level and steady as I put the phone back in its cradle, gripping it hard enough to make my hand shake. As I put it down, it rang, making me jump.

I could hear Carol breathing, fast and shallow.

'I told Denis Tanter to leave us alone,' she said, without even a hello. 'He's gone.'

'What about you, though?' I replied, shoving the phone against my ear as if I could press her closer on the other end of the line.

'I need a few days away, Davey. Work is all over me and I just need a break, a chance to take a breath.'

'Where will you go?' I asked, knowing she wouldn't tell me. It didn't matter. What mattered was that Denis bloody Tanter had lost her and I was filled with a savage joy. I could hear the weariness in her voice. If she had been going to him,

51

she would have had that brittle excitement that marked the beginning of all her affairs. To leave 'us' alone, she'd said. There were times when I did love her, no matter what else I felt. I pressed the phone so hard against the side of my head that it began to hurt.

'I just need a few days away from here,' she said. I waited for something more. I wondered if she had packed a bag. Perhaps if I'd taken the time to look through the bathroom cabinet I might have known the phone call was coming.

'Don't go far,' I said gently. Sometimes I talked to her like you would to a nervous horse, but she didn't seem to mind. I wanted to say that I loved her, to express the sudden warm feeling in my chest when I heard her voice. For once, I couldn't say the words, easy as they are. She never did, and though I told myself it was there in every word and glance she threw me, it still

52

mattered. I'd swallowed so much pride over the years that it washed back into my mouth and burned me. Perhaps I was full at last, and that was why it brimmed over every time I was made to taste a little more defeat, a little more shame. For a moment I hoped she *wouldn't* come back. In a second of phone silence I saw my life going on without the pain and drama. Eventually, she would become a distant memory for someone I used to be. A problem for someone else. All pain goes, remember, even the memories you thought would kill you. Perhaps I would just get in my car and drive away before she came back and pretend to be a normal person for the rest of my life. I might even be happy and live some sort of eerie existence where I didn't have a blood test every month in case she brought home some plague that would strip the flesh off me. It would be a strange sort of life without fear and without hate and without my obsession with her.

I put the phone down without really listening to her say goodbye.

*   *   *

It took about ten minutes of sitting on my own to realize I needed to get out as well. I didn't want to be the one who stayed and waited for her to come back. I didn't want to be on my own, and I certainly didn't want to be there if Denis sent Michael round a second time. That was the thought that really got me moving. She had taken the only suitcase, but there was an old duffel bag in the cupboard over the immersion heater, so I stuffed a few things in that, adding a bar of soap and a half-full can of deodorant. I didn't have the money to bother with a passport. I was thinking of taking a train west, perhaps to spend a few days in Cornwall. I found my good boots and

54

shrugged myself into the coat, moving quickly and controlling a swelling sense of panic.

I opened the door just as I became aware of a moving shadow behind the glass. I'd been thinking about her, and as the lock clicked I realized someone was standing there, looking in. They'd watched me pat pockets for keys and open the duffel over and over to shove some last item into the depths.

They seem to move at a different speed, these people. If someone tries to push his way into a house in a film, the door is likely to slam in their face. Denis just walked in as if it was his own house, though his expression showed what he thought of the place. His shoulder knocked into me and then Michael came in behind, pressing his left hand against my chest and holding me against the wall without the slightest difficulty. I might have struggled if they'd given me a little warning, but it was just too quick and too casual.

As Denis disappeared into the lounge, Michael shook his head almost apologetically. I came to life then in a rush of fear adrenalin, yanking at his fingers to break his grip. The little scrap of garden and freedom was so near I couldn't bear to have the door close and be stuck inside with them. Michael pulled me back from the open doorway and shut it with his other arm, nodding to himself as he heard the click. The hall was darker with him blocking the light.

'Where is she?' Denis demanded, coming back from the kitchen. I didn't reply. For a moment, the strangeness of having him in my house was just too much. I'd seen him last at a New Year's Eve party with balloons and a Scotsman. I remembered his face, but to have him just stand there and talk like we knew each other was surreal.

'I'll call the police,' I said.

Denis raised his eyebrows in something approaching surprise.

'Michael said you don't scare easy,' he said. 'I can't see it, myself.' I glanced sideways at Michael, but his face was blank. No chat from him, or demands to be given whisky. In the great man's presence he was solid business, a professional.

I still said nothing, so Denis gestured for me to be brought along. I found myself being marched into my own kitchen once more. I had a sick feeling that they were going to kill me. For a moment I imagined Carol coming back in a few days, and I'm ashamed to say I took pleasure in the guilt she would feel.

The whisky bottle was still where I had left it, and Denis poured himself a glass of it, taking a sip as he faced me. If I'd planned ahead, I realized I could have laced it with some poison, like in an Agatha Christie book. Honestly, though, where would I have got hold of a decent poison?

He'd have tasted weedkiller, surely? The trouble with that sort of thing is that you end up in prison for life. No matter how things turned out, I wasn't going to let that happen.

Michael snapped his fingers in front of my nose. 'Pay attention and answer the question,' he snapped.

My mind had wandered again, preferring vagueness to the actual reality of waiting to be murdered.

'I don't know where she's gone,' I said. Some part of me had been listening and that was what Denis had asked. 'She's gone away,' I added. I wanted to answer their questions. I wanted the conversation to go on and on, all day if they liked. I didn't want to imagine what would happen when the talking stopped.

'Tell me, David,' Denis said, pulling up the other chair and sitting down. 'Tell me why your wife can't bear to think of leaving you?'

I blinked at him, trying to look as if I was giving his question some serious thought. Only Carol would find me, and she might not be back for days.

'I don't know. She loves me,' I replied. Denis was not a pleasant-looking man to stare at. His skin was flushed and his eyes were flat and cold. His freckles stood out on the pale, bony head, and for an instant I could only see them, like a web of dots on his face.

'Are you cruel to her, David?' he said to me suddenly, almost in a whisper. I could feel him tense as he watched me. He really wanted to know. Poor sod never understood her.

'She's the only thing I value in the world,' I said, leaning closer to him. The truth of this was somehow clear, and Denis shifted uncomfortably. I wondered what his own meat and veg wife had been like. Did he have red-haired little kids with bony faces and hard laughter? Carol was a force of nature compared to his sort of home. I could almost sympathize with what he'd been through.

'You should walk away from this mess,' I told him as he stared. 'She needs me, so I stay. Anything else, any*one* else—they're just strangers.'

I could see he was struggling with some internal argument. He practically shook with irritation and he knocked back the glass of poison-free whisky without seeming to taste it. I heard the bottle clink on the glass as he refilled. I didn't much like the prospect of him getting drunk in my kitchen.

Denis turned round in his seat. 'Are you wearing gloves, Michael?' he asked.

I glanced up to see that Michael was. Denis too had a pair, and I had a sudden sense of dropping from a great height. I don't think I've ever heard something more frightening than that casual question. When Denis turned back to me, I had to hold my hands together on the table

60

to stop them shaking.

'I could make you vanish, David. No husband for her to come home to, understand? Perhaps there would be room then for a man who's more than some weird little parasite. You don't even work, do you, David? You just sit here and spend the money she makes for you. Does that make you feel like a man, David?'

'She would never trust you if I disappeared,' I said slowly. 'She knows you sent Michael the first time. She'll know it was you.' I liked the way this was going and began to warm to the theme. 'She'll hate you if you even bruise me, Mr Tanter. You should have that clear in your head. I can't see a happy ending here unless you just leave.'

He sat back and seemed to ponder this for a while.

'I see what you mean, Mike. He sits there as cool as you like with his arse out in the wind.' I saw Michael smile behind Denis's back. I wasn't completely sure what the phrase meant either, by the way. If it meant vulnerable, that was about right.

Denis stood up, and I felt a spike of sudden hope that he was going to take my advice. He nodded to me.

'You are a sick little man, David. You've turned a wonderful woman into a twisted, fragile . . . I don't know what she is. You might be right about killing you, or it might be the one thing she needs to really wash you off her *skin*, you know what I mean? Just seeing you sitting there looking so smug makes me angry, David. I think you have a hold over her, like those men who beat women and somehow they still come back. I don't understand it. However, I'm not the sort to walk away from things I don't understand, David. I am a *stubborn* man.'

He said it like it was something he'd said a hundred times before, like he was proud of it. I could only stare blankly at him as he walked around Michael and stood at the other end of the kitchen. The room felt cramped with those two blocking the door.

'I'll stay to watch, Mike, if you don't mind,' Denis said.

'How far do you want me to go?' Michael asked, his eyes on mine.

Denis thought for a moment.

'I'll want to have another crack at this when she comes back, so keep it all under his clothes, all right? Teach him something. Break a couple of fingers, but hide the rest.'

I began to yell then, though I knew the neighbours would all be at work. There was no one to help me.

CHAPTER FIVE

I managed to get myself to Brighton General hospital to have my hand splinted. I thought they'd ask me all sorts of difficult questions, but they simply made me wait for six hours just to be told that the X-rays showed two broken fingers. The first thing I'd said to the nurse on reception was, 'I have two broken fingers,' but I didn't mind. They had given me painkillers, and I've always liked the building. It used to be a workhouse in Victorian times, and I like that sense of history. Anyway, it was warm inside and there was a machine to get cups of orange-coloured tea. After all the trouble I'd had getting there, I made the most of it. Steering with one hand isn't a problem, but *changing gear* and steering is a nightmare.

I think if anyone had been nice to

me I might have asked for help, or gone to the police, perhaps. The doctors were too busy to want more than a glance at someone with my kind of problems. Even the nurse who did the bandaging didn't ask how it had happened. She was flustered and tired and she had a bright line of sweat where her hair met her forehead. I found my gaze focusing on it while she worked on me. It must be a strange thing to spend your day with people who have been really hurt. They say policemen think everyone is a criminal. I wonder if doctors think everyone is just a bag of skin and bones waiting to burst apart all over them. I saw some blood on the linoleum floor while I was there, though it was cleaned up so I stopped my mental letter to the local paper.

I think it was then that I thought of writing to my brother. I was a bit woozy from the painkillers and I had a prescription for more. There was a small leak of acid into my mouth, but when I swallowed it back it stayed down, to my relief. I couldn't go home and I couldn't find my car keys. I knew I'd driven to the hospital, but the damn things had walked somewhere between the reception and the waiting room and the X-ray waiting room and the X-ray machine and the nurses' station and all the other places they'd sent me. I couldn't bear to get up and begin the search for them.

'Excuse me, miss, have you seen a set of car keys? I was here just a minute ago'—over and over. If they were lost, I would walk home, or call the RAC and pretend to be a young woman on her own so they'd come quickly. I was past caring about anything.

At the pharmacy on the ground floor I exchanged the prescription for a bottle of pills and bought paper, stamps and envelopes from a little newsagent in the same patient-friendly grouping. Hospital is *dull*. I saw a bald cancer kid and wondered how they get through the days. Time moves really slowly in there.

I couldn't send the first letter I wrote. It was one of those you do to get everything clear in your head. It was angry and I swore a lot. If I'd sent that, my brother might have had me committed to the mental wing back at Brighton General. There is a real difference between committing yourself and having someone else do it for you. Apart from the way you are treated, the main thing is that you can walk out when you see the nurses violently restraining someone as they scream and spit blood. If you are sectioned and sent there, even for something as harmless as depression and a suicide watch, you can't get out—you're in the system and they lose all interest in how you feel or what you need.

I tore the letter into tiny shreds in

case someone had the time to glue it back together in between emptying the bins of a hospital. Even though I knew it was stupid, I still made sure the pieces ended up in two separate bins.

I kept the second try short. It said I was having trouble with Carol and I didn't know what to do. If you'd asked me then what I was hoping for, I probably couldn't have told you. I couldn't handle Denis Tanter and I couldn't see a way out. That's when you ask for help. You don't know what the help is going to be. If you did, you could probably do it on your own. I put it in the hospital postbox and walked stiffly away from it without looking back. It was done. He would either come or he wouldn't.

Two days later he left a message on the answering machine to say he was on the way. Nothing more, just ten seconds of his voice while I sat and watched the machine. Hearing him brought back a lot of unpleasant memories. I took my half-empty bottle of Laphroaig to keep me warm, put on my best black suit and wrote a letter to Carol. I left it on the kitchen table where she would see it if she came back. After that I walked down to the beach, and when it was dark I stood on the edge of the black sea, looking out. I finished the whisky and scooped up a little salt water to cut the taste of it. It was as bitter as I was, and it was around then that I stopped feeling the cold and walked into the water.

I don't know how long I stood there before he found me. He'd read the letter on the table. I knew he would.

*   *   *

I told him all of it as we walked back along the dark streets of Brighton. The wind had picked up and I was shivering so he gave me his coat. It smelled of cigars and his aftershave, which wasn't one I knew. It was a better coat than I have ever owned and I could feel its weight and softness like the first touches of guilt.

He hardly commented as we walked together, asking just an occasional question about Denis or Michael, my impressions of them. I had to tell him more than I wanted to about Carol or it would have seemed nonsense. It came out in pieces, and once he looked at me and shook his head in slow amazement.

'And you want her back?' he said. I hated him then.

I told him everything I could remember, anything that might help him to understand the two men who had come into my life and pushed me to desperation. I tried not to think that I was considering murder or, at the least, allowing murder in my name. I wanted them out of my life, and somewhere during the second beating in my kitchen I had stopped caring how it happened. Perhaps it was when my first finger was bent far enough to snap. Shame leads to rage in men, did you know that? If you want to see a white-hot tantrum, try humiliating a man, especially in public. Try making one afraid and then laughing about it.

I was too cold to take pleasure in the conversation with my brother, but I could see that he did. Even without his coat he seemed too full of interest to feel the wind off the sea. He moved his hands in sharp cutting gestures when he talked, and he laughed at my description of Michael, making me repeat details so that he would know either of them on sight.

I hadn't realized how much planning would go into removing two men from the world. My brother was my single extra card, my one advantage that no one else knew about. He'd parked a mile from the house and walked. No one had a clue where he was and no one would ever be able to connect him to anything that happened. For a few days at least, he was going to enjoy himself. No guilt, no conscience.

We sat at the kitchen table and he swore when I told him there wasn't anything left to drink in the house. I'd thrown the empty bottle of Laphroaig into the sea before he came, a better splash in imagination than it actually was.

'You've seen Michael alone, so they're not joined at the hip,' he said, thinking aloud. 'It would be easier for me if I can catch each one by himself.'

'But if you make a mistake and get caught, the other one will kill me.'

'Or you'd kill him, little brother. Don't think I don't know you,' he said, with a strange glint in his eye. I remembered him kicking the limp head of the man outside the club in Camden and I shuddered.

'I'd try,' I promised him. He nodded.

'You'd do it to save Carol, I know you would.'

I didn't like him mentioning her. I wanted to think about the problem, not what would happen afterwards. I didn't want her to know anything about it. Denis would just be found somewhere and his death put down to one of his unpleasant business partners. No one would suspect me and no one would know my brother had even been in Brighton. I wanted it clean.

'Mind you, the only way to get him somewhere we can prepare is to tell him Carol wants to see him. A pub car park at night, say. When he gets fed up waiting, he comes out in the dark and I do something very violent for ten or fifteen seconds.' He seemed to be enjoying the prospect and I had to swallow hard to clear the burning trail that surged up under my tongue.

'It's too risky. You can't predict when he comes out so there could be a family standing by his car, or a group of drunks peeing in the gutter—witnesses. Even if you managed to . . . stop one of them, the other one would shout, or run. We'd never get away with it. It's madness to think you could—'

'All right, Davey, don't get in a froth,' he said curtly, cutting me off. 'You might run down to the off-licence before it closes and buy me something stronger than orange squash. I might get the ideas flowing then.' He smiled then, so cold and self-assured that I wanted to throw up. 'Best to do it here, anyway, in this house,' he said, looking around the kitchen. 'We'll get them where we can control things. He's a man who employs a thug and breaks fingers. You'll get away with a self-defence plea and they'll never even know you had help.'

'Are you wearing gloves?' I asked

him, suddenly. He was.

'That's more like it, Davey boy. Now you're thinking.'

The front door clicked open and I jumped to my feet in fear. My brother didn't move and when he saw who was standing there he just smiled, his eyes half hooded with interest.

'Hello, Carol love,' he said. 'Did you bring anything to drink?'

*   *   *

I saw her flicker a gaze to me and then back to him, wondering what we had been discussing. She looked rested and she'd had her hair cut. There was a new bag on her shoulder and she looked as beautiful as always. New shoes too, I noticed, when my eyes dropped at last.

'It's always nice to see one of Davey's family,' she said coolly, her eyes making a complete lie of it. I could feel the dislike between them

75

and I wondered if they'd fight if I left to get whisky. I realized there would be at least one witness to the fact that my brother was in Brighton, and my stomach churned. Why couldn't she have spent a few more days discovering her inner child or whatever the hell it was she got up to on these trips?

'I'd better get to bed,' she said, staging a yawn. 'I'll see you tomorrow.' My brother didn't look up, and when she'd gone I realized she hadn't even asked about my splinted hand. She hadn't seen it, I was half certain. She'd expected a welcome and instead there we were, looking . . . well, looking like a couple of conspirators planning a murder.

My brother leaned forward and spoke in what was barely a murmur. 'Having her here is going to be a problem,' he said. Then he grinned. 'However, this isn't a bank robbery and I don't need to spend ages planning it. Just make sure she's well clear when we get your two friends into this kitchen one more time.'

'She'll tell the police you were here,' I said, just as quietly. I couldn't meet his eyes, but it had to be considered. The police wouldn't be looking at a lone man defending himself against two vicious career thugs. They would be looking for a lone man's brother, mysteriously vanished from Brighton the very day after a double murder. When I did look up, he was frowning, turning it over and over in his mind.

After a while of me watching him, he said, 'Why don't you go and get that bloody whisky while I'm thinking?'

I went.

CHAPTER SIX

I came sharply out of sleep, jerked from a dream by some noise she made as she dressed. My first view was of her standing in bra and knickers, pulling on her skirt. She'd been asleep by the time I had come up the night before, or at least pretending to be. She saw me move in the dressing-table mirror, and we looked at each other for a long moment. I saw her eyes drift down to my splinted hand, large and white on the duvet. A T-shirt covered the other bruises.

'I tore two fingernails off, changing a tyre,' I said, watching her wince. 'You should see what it looks like.'

'No thanks, Davey. I have to get going.'

It was half an hour earlier than she usually left and I couldn't help my glance at the alarm clock. She had the grace to look away as I did, straightening the collar of her blouse in the mirror. I guessed she wanted to be out of the house before my brother was up. Sometimes I can read her too easily.

'He's only visiting for a day or two,' I said.

She nodded, her mouth a tight line and pale without her lipstick. With a few more brisk movements she finished her routine and left the room, leaving just a faint touch of perfume on the air. I liked to watch the change, from sleepy tangles to smart estate agent, all polished and shining.

My brother had come up with the lie for the broken fingers. If I'd told her about Denis coming back she might have gone to the police, or worse, called the man himself from her office. She still might call him, of course, but I believed Denis when he told me she had ended it, or at least I believed his anger and hurt. Funny that. I wouldn't have believed her.

It was a small risk, though, and we knew we would have to act quickly. Even as she closed the front door behind her, I heard my brother turn the shower on. It was going to be today. By the time she came home from work, our little problem would be handled.

I pulled on a dressing gown when I heard the shower squeak to a stop. It was an odd moment to come out onto the landing and see him there. I think the last time I'd seen him with a towel around his waist was when we were kids. He looked a lot stronger, I noticed. He wasn't carrying any fat and he looked as if he kept himself very fit. It is easier for men with high levels of testosterone, you know. They enjoy exercise more than other men, right up to the heart attack that kills them. I folded my arms across the front of my dressing gown and nodded to him. We had planned everything, but

I could feel my heart pounding at an insane speed.

'Are you ready, little brother? No second thoughts?' he asked me, amusement in his voice. He didn't seem nervous at all.

'No second thoughts,' I said.

*   *   *

We moved fast after that. It was just possible that Denis might hear Carol had come back to work. For all we knew, he walked by the office every morning, or paid the secretary to pass on any news of her. It was probably just nerves, but it didn't hurt to move things along as quickly as possible. The way my brother worked things out, we had one chance to get this right. Even with Carol knowing he was in Brighton, it would still work, he assured me. He'd been to court over Bobby Penrith and got away with it. He would again.

I sat in the kitchen with the phone on the table in front of me, just looking at it and going over what we'd planned in my head. It was all very well to work out the details in my imagination, but when I picked up that phone and dialled, it would really begin. After that it would be like stepping off a cliff—it just doesn't matter if you change your mind halfway through.

'Try it on me first,' my brother demanded. It was the first sign of nervousness I'd seen from him. I shook my head, going over what we'd planned to say. It would bring Denis running, I knew it would.

I saw him pour a glass of the whisky I'd bought the night before. I jerked back as his hand moved, but most of it still caught me in the face. I cried out in anger, remembering Michael doing just the same.

'What the hell are you doing?' I said, holding one eye closed against the sting.

'Now you're ready to make the call,' he said, laughing at my expression. 'You were just a little too relaxed before. Go on. Do it.'

I glanced at the scrap of paper beside the phone with the number of Denis Tanter on it. One call to directory enquiries had given me the last thing I needed.

I punched in the numbers and took a deep breath.

'WT Limited,' it was a woman's voice, not one I knew. A secretary, maybe. I kept calm. This was the number I'd been given.

'Get Denis Tanter on the line,' I said, slurring slightly. The whisky fumes helped a little, strangely enough.

'Who is this?' she asked. I felt acid flood into my mouth and I grimaced at the taste of it.

'Just you go and get him. Tell him to come and clear up his messes, all right? Tell him . . .'

I heard the change-over going on

83

and I was ready for it when the new voice came.

'Who *is* this?' Michael. That was all I'd wanted.

'You bastard,' I sneered at him. 'She's dead and it's because of Denis bloody Tanter, isn't it? You go to hell, you . . .' I trailed off, snuffling drunkenly as if I were weeping, or pressing a hand against my face. Give the man a chance to respond.

'Davey? Who's dead? Not Carol? Davey, is that you?' Perfect. I could hear the fear in his voice. It was just the beginning of what he had coming.

'Pills!' I spat the word at the phone, leaving a trail of whisky and spittle on it. 'You pushed and you pushed, didn't you, Michael? You and Denis. You pushed us, and now Carol's dead. I swear, I'm—'

My brother took the phone from me and pressed the button that ended the call. His face was a study in quiet awe.

84

'That was just right, Davey boy. That should bring them running,' he said. I nodded at him, wiping roughly at my mouth.

'We'd better get ready,' he muttered, dropping the phone back into its cradle with a clatter. He'd brought a bag in from the car and I watched as he removed an eighteen-inch length of iron bar that I couldn't help but pick up. It fitted the hand very well indeed. I took a swing with it and imagined it cracking into a skull.

To my surprise, the bag went on to reveal a number of other pieces of pipe and various other tools.

'For afterwards,' he said. 'It explains why you had a weapon to hand in a kitchen, doesn't it?' With a grim smile, he opened the cupboard under the sink and showed me how he'd unscrewed the plastic tubing. 'They'll probably never ask, but I thought, what the hell. If they do, all they'll find is a little plumbing job. I was in the middle of it when I had to go out and look for a place that sells another piece the same as the one I cracked so artfully. While I'm away, you have a visit from two men who have threatened you before.'

I looked at him and I swear he was calmer than I was. In just a few minutes Denis Tanter was going to come charging into my house for the third time. I pulled a carton of milk out of the fridge and drank from it to quiet my stomach.

My brother reached into his jacket and showed me a vicious-looking knife.

'They come armed with this. It's sold in any hardware shop in the country. Not surprisingly, you panic and swing at them with a bit of pipe. You call the police, and before they arrive I come back. We handle their questions together.'

'You think it will work?' I asked him.

He shrugged. 'I don't think it will

even go to court. Two against one? Self-defence will see you clear of it, Davey. No problem at all. You just trust me and we'll see it through, all right?'

I looked him in the eyes, and for a moment I could feel tears come. I nodded, turning away, knowing he had seen.

'Now concentrate, Davey. They should be here any minute. You have the easy bit. You just sit down in the kitchen like we planned it. Have a drink, if you have to, just look miserable.'

As I sat down, my brother went to the front door and left it on the latch.

'Remind me to break the lock in afterwards,' he said as he came back to the kitchen and stood behind the door. He hefted the metal bar in his hand and I couldn't look at him.

Outside, we heard a car engine roaring closer, being driven too fast. It screeched to a halt. I took a deep breath.

CHAPTER SEVEN

Denis Tanter came into my home at 9.28 in the morning. I looked up at the wall clock, so I know. He hit the front door so hard that I think he would have smashed the lock right off if we'd locked it. It hammered back against the wall and then bounced off his shoulder as he bulled his way in. I'd read him right, I was pleased to see. I'd told my brother he wasn't the type to send Michael in first, not if his blood was up. It didn't seem to worry my brother, but I wanted Denis in first. He was the dangerous one, not his man. I'd known that from the beginning.

He hadn't the faintest idea what was going on. I could see that from the moment he caught sight of me in the kitchen. I was looking pathetic, with tear trails down my face and an expression of stunned fear. It wasn't hard to fake when you know someone is going to die in the next few minutes and it could very well be you.

'Where is she?' he roared at me. He was flushed with high emotion, and for an awful moment I thought he was going to go charging upstairs to search the bedrooms for her. I shook my head and gestured vaguely across the kitchen. He scowled at me and I saw his fists rise as he stepped inside the door. Michael was a shadow in the hall behind him, but I could only watch Denis as my brother struck. God, he was fast. You've never seen anything like it.

It wasn't a crunch. It sounded like a bag of flour bursting, a sort of soft thump. Staring straight at Denis, I swear I saw the end of the bar sink into his head before it came back. The anger, the light, everything that called itself Denis Tanter went out in an instant. My brother hit him again as he began to fall, and then once more. I couldn't help remembering the way he'd kicked and kicked at the man in Camden and I knew there was at least one other body in his wake. There are moments in our lives when the lies we tell ourselves just fall away. This was one of them, for me.

My brother ignored Michael as the man stood stunned in the doorway, his mouth open in horror. Instead, my older brother looked at *me* and grinned. He didn't seem to care that Michael was there. I watched in sick fascination as my brother nudged Denis with his foot. The body twitched and I thought I might lose my breakfast.

'Dead, or a vegetable, no doubt about it,' he said, and I swear he chuckled. I'd rarely seen him happier. Perhaps you can see now why I've always been frightened of him. It wasn't so much what he did, but what he was capable of.

Michael began to move and I was

pleased I couldn't see my brother's expression when he turned back to finish the job. There are sharks in the world and, like Bobby Penrith before him, Michael just wasn't prepared to meet a bigger one in my kitchen, on that day. I saw him reach into his jacket for some sort of weapon. My brother didn't trouble to stop him. He just smacked the bar against the side of Michael's head, breaking something inside. Michael dropped almost as fast as Denis had, as the signals from his brain to his legs were interrupted.

I came to my feet in a sort of trance, feeling only pity for Michael. He was a hired man, after all, but I'd sat and watched him twist my fingers right round and I didn't call out to save him, even if I could have.

The man Denis had hired to cause a little fear in those he dealt with had always struck me as large, not fast, but strong. It was surprising to see how my brother loomed over him as he hit him again. Fear shrinks you somehow, and courage swells you up larger than you really are. I've noticed that before.

I'd found my own bit of pipe in the plumber's bag my brother had brought with him. I don't think he heard me coming, but even if he did he didn't expect me to smash it down on him with all the strength of years of fear and hatred. I'd seen him break a skull just a few moments before and I'm pleased to say that I did it just as neatly as he did. I killed my brother as he hit Michael for a second time, so that the two blows sounded almost together. He fell sideways, sprawling over the broken bodies. He didn't move and I almost left it at that, but he'd seemed to think two hits were needed to be sure. I held my breath and brought the pipe down again onto his crown, with all the force I could. It was already soft and I felt it give. His eyes were open and I don't think he could still feel anything. The first one had been pretty hard.

There was some blood dripping, but it wasn't too bad. Most of it was on them and spattered across the kitchen. It looked just as he'd said it would, like a violent scene of a fight.

I stood looking at them for a while, I can't say how long. My stomach betrayed me, of course, so I wasted a few minutes vomiting into the sink and wondering if I should get rid of it or leave it as a reasonable reaction to such horror. I left it, in the end. The police would come asking eventually and I knew they could be persistent. My brother was right about one thing, though. The self-defence works even better with him dead. I had an idea that I might even end up as a hero.

When my stomach had stopped going into spasm, I sat down at the kitchen table and poured a last toast to the three of them.

I raised my glass to my brother.

'Here's to growing up, old son. You should never have slept with her,' I told him. 'That was just a little too much for me. Still, it's all forgotten now.'

I found myself chuckling, and it was an effort to stop. I wondered if he even knew I'd found out, that Carol had thrown it at me in one of our fights. He wasn't the sort to feel guilt. I've no doubt that it was just a thrill for him to find a beautiful woman willing to waste an afternoon, no matter who she was married to. It was strange to see the way they acted around each other after I knew. Whatever memory they'd made had gone a bit sour, I could see that. Perhaps she'd refused a second round, or he'd refused her. It didn't matter to me much, not any more.

It was strange to see the bodies in my own kitchen. I'd seen it in my imagination enough times, but to have actually reached the point was like time standing still and more than a little bit frightening. Reality is like that, I've found.

I'd worked out most of the details while I was standing in the freezing sea waiting for my brother to read the note I'd left for Carol and come and get me. I remember worrying that he might have had an accident or a flat tyre, and all my effort would have been wasted. I *knew* seeing me there would get him on my side. I was always his blind spot, his little brother. I don't think he cared about another living soul. I'm not ashamed to say there were tears in my eyes for a while, looking at him. Brothers are close.

I'd hardly needed to persuade him after he found me standing in a foot of dark water, trying hard to imagine what it must be like to commit suicide. Really, it couldn't have gone better, it really couldn't. My debts were all paid, and I sort of hoped Bobby Penrith knew they had been.

The police would accept my story,

95

if I left enough shocked blanks in it. It was simple enough, after all. I'd let him guide me where I wanted to go. Just two brothers fixing a pipe in a kitchen and being attacked by a violent pair of criminals. I wondered if I should explain about Carol to the police. No. I didn't want them knowing I had any kind of motive. I thought they would believe Denis was obsessed with her without knowing he'd tried her out a few times as well. It worked very nicely.

I walked outside the front door, pulling it shut behind me. The neighbours were at work as always, so there wouldn't be any witnesses the police could interrogate. It took a couple of thumps with my shoulder to break the lock. No doubt it would be another bruise to show the police when I told them how Denis Tanter had tortured me. Perfect.

I remembered to put my pipe in Michael's hand while I was scattering the contents of the plumber's bag over the kitchen floor. I found a knife in his other pocket, the one he'd been reaching for when my brother knocked him down. After a bit of thought, I let him hold it in his other hand, taking care with my own prints.

There were a lot of things to remember. There would be blood spatter on my clothes, but I thought that would be fine. I could see it would be suspicious if there wasn't in such a small space, with three men beaten to death. I was pleased with how clearly I was thinking.

When I sat down at last, I had the phone in my hand to call them. I'd done everything I could and I thought, yes, Davey, you will get away with this. I said the words aloud, even, while they all just lay there and bled. That was one surprise. No matter what you've heard, the sheer volume of blood is a shock. It just doesn't seem possible to have that much in you. It's not true that dead men don't bleed, either. These ones did, for a while at least. The kitchen was covered in the stuff and I still can't believe just how sticky it is when it gets on you. Different shades of red as well.

I had thought I could handle Denis Tanter, just as I've dealt with a few other men over the years. When I realized I couldn't, I thought I would let my brother handle him. It was just an idle thought at first of how nice it would be if both of the bastards killed each other. I hadn't really thought about afterwards, though. If there had ever been a place to think about afterwards, it was that kitchen with its pool of blood and a smell I never want to get near again.

It's not often you have an opportunity like that, you see. Yes, I could beat the court case, if it even went to court. The Crown Prosecution Service has to decide there's a case they can win, and my plea of self-defence against those boys was going to be a beauty. I could walk away, but then there was Carol. Did I really want to walk away with her? I couldn't help but think that if she had been in the middle of this mess when Denis and Michael arrived, perhaps she too would be lying there and I would be free. Really free, as opposed to the shadow of it I'd been enjoying for a few brief moments.

It was clearly a day for new beginnings. Instead of the police, I rang her and told her I was going to take all her sleeping pills in one go. I put the phone down in the middle of a sentence, then removed its battery. I wasn't worried. I'd work out the details before she got home.